Gilbert GOES OUTSIDE

Colin Thompson & Chris Mould

Lothian
BOOKS

Gilbert was not a happy boy.

He did not like things to change.
Most animals and a lot of people
are like that, but with Gilbert
it was worse.

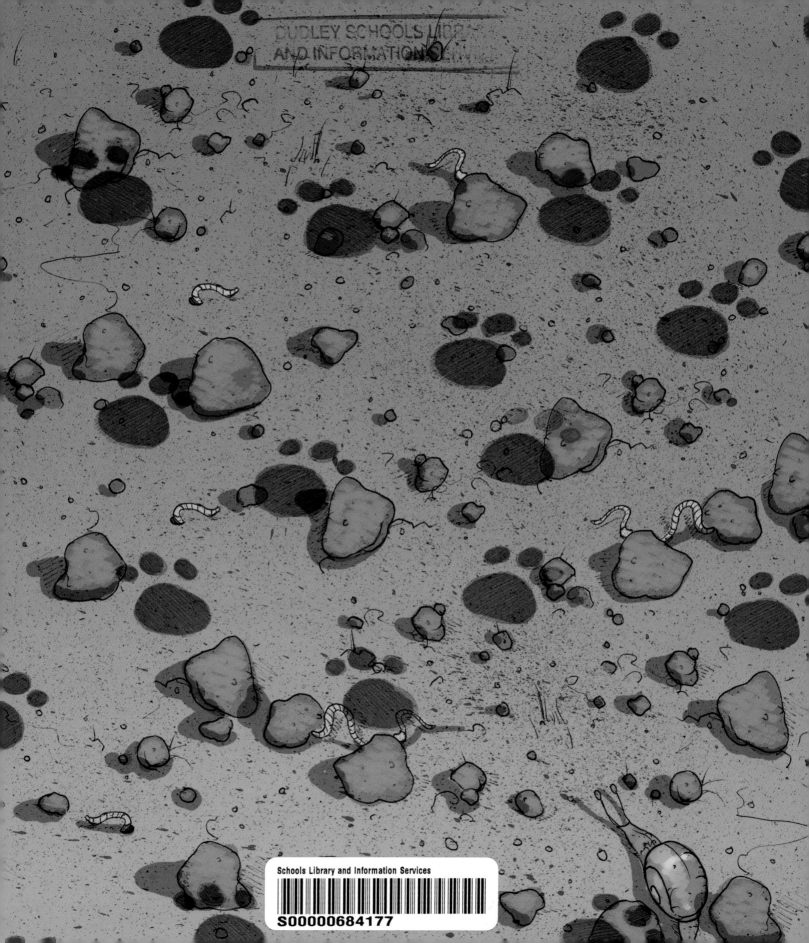

To all fat cats who sometimes get a bit nervous. C.T.

For Sam and Abigail. C.M.

Gilbert Yahoo Morgan-Jones,
Creative Consultant

Visit Colin Thompson's website at
http://www.colinthompson.com

Thomas C. Lothian Pty Ltd
132 Albert Road, South Melbourne, Victoria 3205

Text copyright © Colin Thompson 2005
Illustrations copyright © Chris Mould 2005

First published 2005

National Library of Australia
Cataloguing-in-Publication data:

Thompson, Colin (Colin Edward).

Gilbert goes outside.

For young children.
ISBN 0 7344 0876 5

1. Cats - Juvenile fiction. 2. Fear - Juvenile fiction. I.
Mould, Chris. II. Title.

A823.3

Designed by Chris Mould
Prepress by Print+Publish, Port Melbourne
Printed in China by SNP Leefung

If the lady he called his mum
moved the furniture around
so the armchair was
by the window
and not the door,
it upset him for a week.

One Tuesday his *mum*
made the biggest
change Gilbert had
ever seen.

She left the back door
open and she even said,

'Come on, Gilbert,
let's go into
the garden.'

Gilbert ran under the bed and tried to hide
inside his favourite paper bag.

He'd seen the garden from the veranda and he knew it
was the most frightening thing in the whole wide world.
There were animals out there, and the green carpet
moved around in the wind.

'No way,' said Gilbert, but his mum couldn't understand him. She dragged him out from under the bed and carried him outside.

'I'm going to die. I'm going to die,'
Gilbert cried and closed his eyes.

'Look at the beautiful flowers,
Gilbert, and the lovely sunshine,'
said his mum.

'This is a crazy person,' Gilbert said.
'I'm living with a crazy person.'

Then it got worse.

MUCH WORSE.

His *mum* put him down.
The grass was all around his feet.
It was awful. It really hurt the little soft
bits between his toes which he was always
so careful to keep pink and clean.

'You lie in the sun for a bit,' said his *mum*
and went back into the house,
shutting the door behind her.

'I, no, er, no, HELP!!!!!' Gilbert cried.

He wanted to run under the bed,
but the only bed in the garden was
the flower bed and it was full of
dirty brown stuff.

But it looked dark like under his bed indoors,
so he ran towards it.

The brown stuff stuck between his toes and he sat
under a big green plant wishing cats could cry.

But as often happens when things look bad,
something good came along.
Behind the plants, at the bottom of the fence,
was a paper bag.
Gilbert felt his heart leap with joy.

He was safe.

He had somewhere to hide.

He went over to the bag
and wriggled inside it.

Inside the bag was not like the ones indoors.
The inside of this bag was occupied.
There was a ring of beetroot,
a lettuce leaf, some fried onions,
a bread roll and
half a beefburger.

They took up a lot of room
inside the bag.
So to make enough room
to fit all of him in,
Gilbert ate the beefburger.

Then he fell asleep.

He had a rather scary dream but it wasn't nearly as bad as the dream his tummy had with the second-hand beefburger inside it.

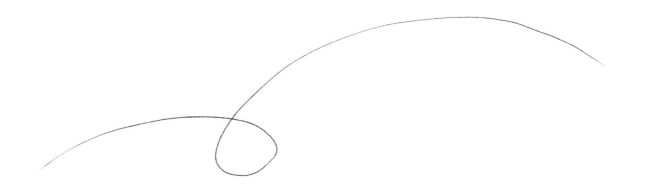

Gilbert woke up feeling very sick.
His stomach was *jumping up and down*
as he staggered across the lawn.

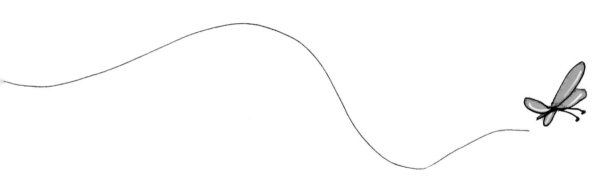

He came to a step and, leaning over it,
he was horribly sick.

At the bottom of the step
there was more grass.

There was also a pile of cat sick.

And under the cat sick was a big black cat who was not happy.

Gilbert had never seen another cat before and was about to say hello when the black cat threw itself at him.

'STUPID,
UGLY,
FAT,
GINGER IDIOT,'
it screamed,
and it bit
Gilbert's
ear.

Gilbert didn't know anything
about fighting and the
black cat bit him all over,
though mostly in his fur,
which he couldn't feel.

Gilbert's mum,
hearing all the
commotion,
raced out to
rescue her
little boy.

'There, there,' she said
as she tucked him into bed.
'Did the nasty black cat
attack *my* poor baby?'

That was almost the final straw.

He had a *tummy* ache, a headache, a sore ear,
dirt between his toes and nextdoor's cat
had bitten him. And, to make it even worse,
nextdoor's cat was a girl.

The final straw was what his Mum said next.
'Gilbert, you're a big boy now. I think it's time
you stopped hiding in paper bags.'

She screwed up all the bags Gilbert had
collected under the bed and threw them
in the rubbish.

In the middle of the night, when everyone was asleep, Gilbert crept back into the garden and sat in the moonlight smelling his old paper bags.

'I wish I was dead,' he said.

But the next morning, when the sun came out, things didn't look so bad.

'I am a big boy,' Gilbert said, 'and I am not afraid of the garden.'

He went outside and lay in the sun.

'FATTY, BUM BUM!' shouted nextdoor's cat through the fence. But Gilbert ignored her.

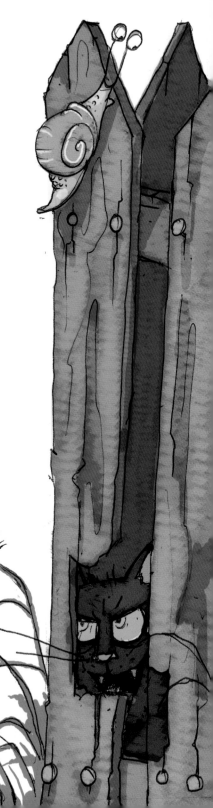

He had other things on his mind.
There was an ache in his heart where
paper bags used to live, an ache he thought
he would never be able to fill.

But then he saw it, standing next to the dustbin.
Big and brown and beautiful.
A dream that made paper bags look pathetic.

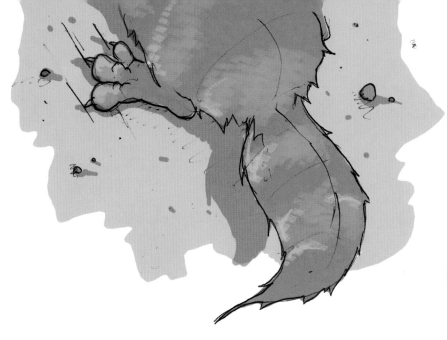

It took him all
morning to drag it
across the lawn and
all lunchtime to
drag it up the steps
into the house.

And it was half past Oprah
by the time he got it safely
jammed under the bed
in the darkest
corner.

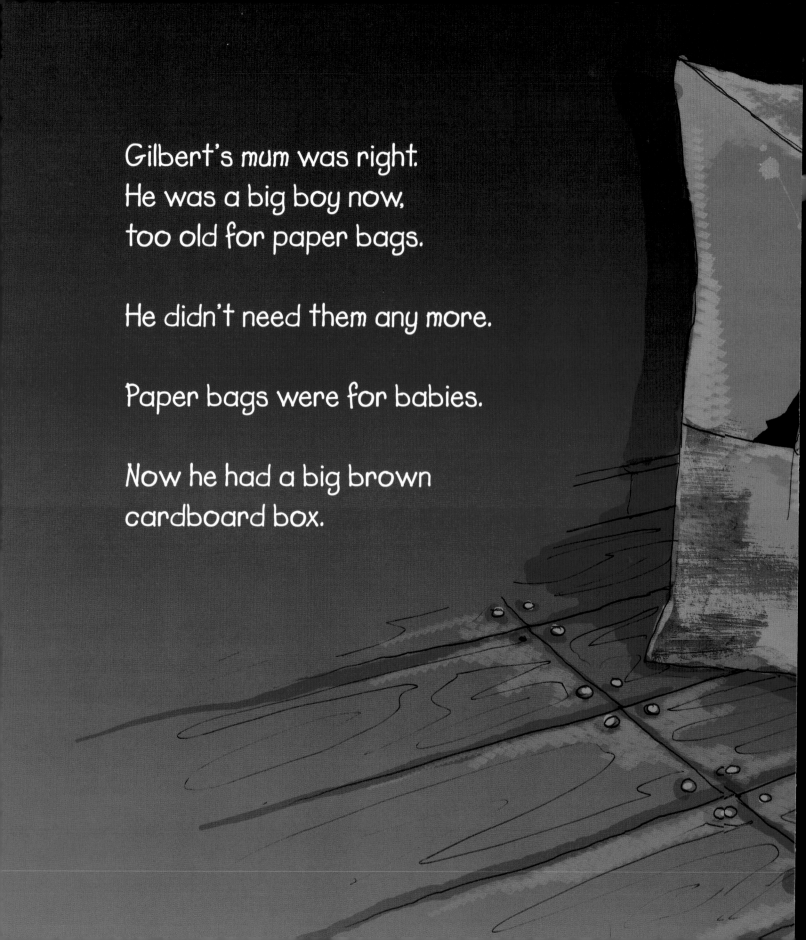

Gilbert's *mum* was right.
He was a big boy now,
too old for paper bags.

He didn't need them any more.

Paper bags were for babies.

Now he had a big brown
cardboard box.

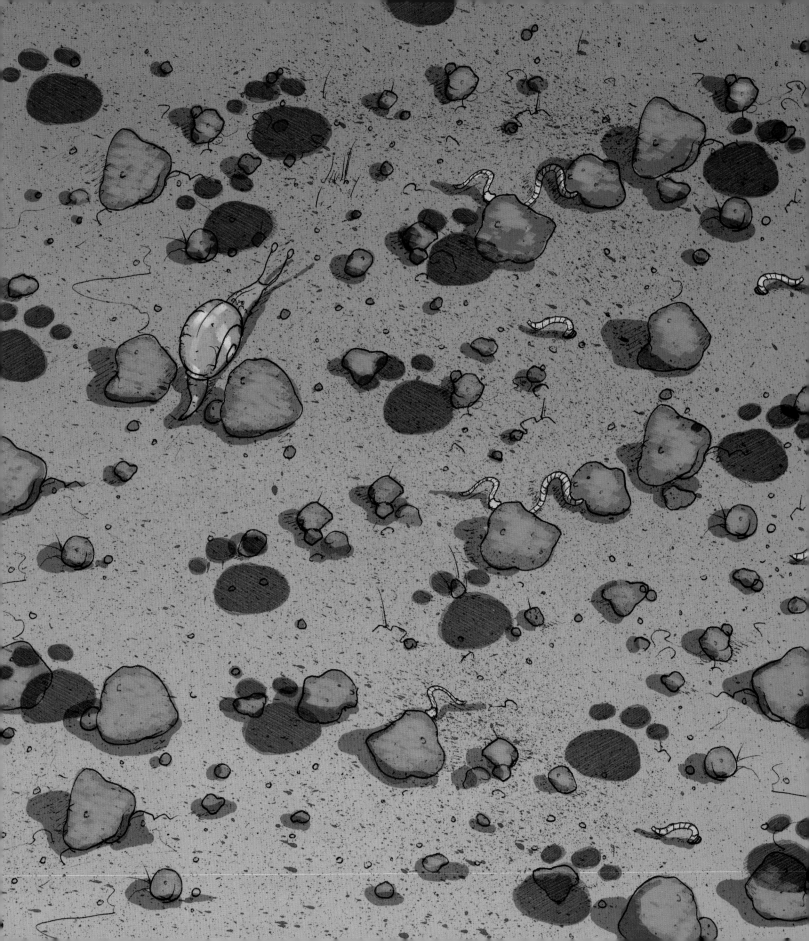